Happy Birthday
Annie!
We love you ♡
XOXO
MoMo, Frank, Shaun, Jack
and Papa

2015

We hope you fall in
love with Shenanigan Boo
as much as we
have. 😊
Julie Gravill

Lacey Grant

2015

Happy Birthday
Anne!
We love you ♥
XOXO
Memo, Frank, Shaun, Zack
and Papa

The Squirrel Named SHENANIGAN BOO

Lacey Grant

Illustrations by Julie Grant

KIDS

BROWN BOOKS KIDS

May we all learn to appreciate the simplicity and beauty in nature.
Thank you for teaching us, Dadums.

To all the kids in my life,
thank you for continuing to inspire me every day.

The Squirrel Named Shenanigan Boo

Brown Books Kids
16250 Knoll Trail Drive, Suite 205
Dallas, Texas 75248
www.BrownBooksKids.com
(972) 381-0009

A New Era in Publishing™

ISBN 978-1-61254-172-3
LCCN 2014938119

Printed in the United States
10 9 8 7 6 5 4 3 2 1

For more information or to contact the author, please go to
www.ShenaniganBoo.com

There once was a squirrel named Shenanigan Boo.
He was just so hungry that he didn't know what to do.

It was a big ol' world,
and he was on his own,
trying to find food,
just peanuts or corn.

You see, he was a spry little guy who always wanted to explore.
He was energetic and excited, ready to see more.

So one day he decided to leave the only farm he knew.
It was spring, and there was just so much to see and do.

Shenanigan Boo set off on his way.
Hopping trees and jumping fences,
he was learning so much each day.

He began to grow lonely
and afraid at times.
Some new things were scary; there were
loud noises, cars, dogs, and power lines.

Suddenly he came upon a garden
with a blue fountain and several trees:
a Japanese maple, a pecan,
and an old hickory.

There lived a quiet man
with white hair and a large hat.
Watering his plants and whistling a tune,
on a bucket he sat.

The squirrel decided to hang around
for a while hiding out in a tree.
Watching and waiting,
maybe this was the place to be.

When evening fell,
the man started hammering and drilling.
Shenanigan Boo wondered
what he might be building.

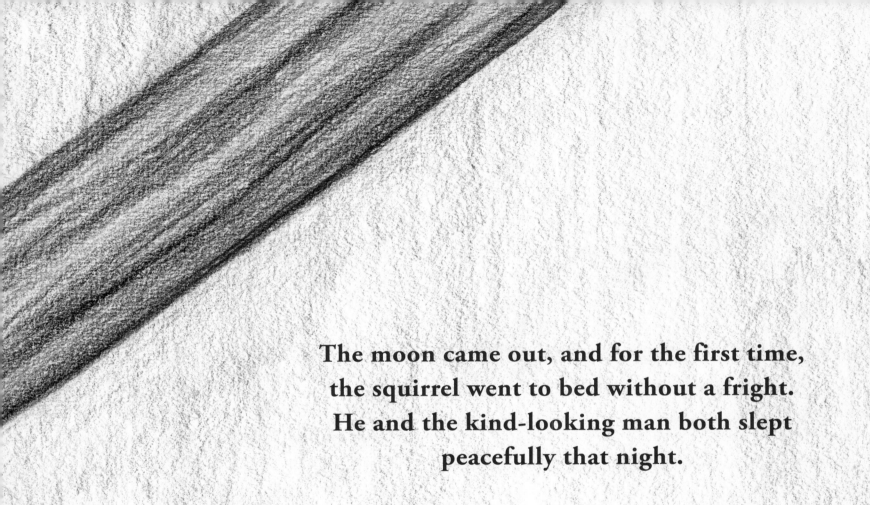

The moon came out, and for the first time,
the squirrel went to bed without a fright.
He and the kind-looking man both slept
peacefully that night.

When the sun rose
and all of the birds started to sing,
Shenanigan Boo saw
the most amazing thing—

the man with the hat
was putting out seeds,
in the new birdhouse
he had been making all week.

As Shenanigan looked around
as far as he could see—
there were birdhouses, butterfly houses,
and wait—could it be?

A new squirrel house had been placed
up in the pecan tree!

It had peanuts and corn,
what a wonderful sight.
He knew he had found a home
that was just right.

Shenanigan looked at the man, who tipped his hat as if he knew,
how grateful the squirrel was for the house and the food.

The squirrel stood on his hind legs on the fence.
He knew that he and the man would be best of friends.

The squirrel met a bird,
a gold finch named Finnegan;
he began hopping trees and jumping fences.
It was so much fun to play again.

He then remembered
what his mom used to say:
"Shenanigan Boo, don't be frightened,
things work out always."

About the Author

Lacey Grant works as a pediatric speech therapist in Fort Worth, Texas, where she resides with her husband and two children. Lacey and Julie Grant are lucky enough to be sisters-in-law.

About the Illustrator

Julie Grant lives in Fort Worth, Texas, with her husband and three children. She spends her days teaching middle school art students at All Saints' Episcopal School. She enjoys the happy diversion of illustrating for her wonderful sister-in-law, Lacey.